Bats

Written by
Stephen Rickard

Contents

1	What are bats?	4
2	What do bats look like?	6
3	Where do bats live?	8
4	What do bats eat?	10
5	Can bats 'see' with their ears?	12
6	Can bats hurt us?	14
7	Index	16

What are bats?

Bats are animals.

There are many kinds of bats.

What do bats look like?

A bat looks a bit like a large mouse, but it has wings.

The wings are made of skin. Bats do not have feathers. Bats can fly, but they are not birds.

Where do bats live?

Bats like to live in places such as caves and trees.

Bats sleep in the daytime. They sleep hanging upside-down. At night they come out to feed.

Some people make bat boxes. These are homes for bats.

Bat boxes

What do bats eat?

Most bats eat insects. Many bats eat fruit.

Some bats feed on small animals, such as frogs.

One kind of bat feeds on blood!

This kind of bat feeds on blood.

Can bats 'see' with their ears?

Bats do not have very good eyes.
They cannot see well.

So bats use their ears to know
where things are around them.

They do this very well.

In this way, they can 'see' in the dark.

Can bats hurt us?

No. Bats can look scary, but they do not hurt people.

Index

bat boxes   8, 9

birds   6

blood   10

caves   8

feathers   6

frogs   10

fruit   10

insects   10

skin   6

trees   8

wings   6